curved

This book is dedicated with love
to Debora Johnson-Ross
and Loretta Johnson,
to Douglas L. Johnson Jr.
and Sonia King-Johnson,
and to the memory of
Earl "Pete" Taylor Jr.,
John Taylor,
and Jaunine Clark
—D. J.

To my grandmothers,
the late Ruby G. Ransome
and the late Rosa Lee Williams
—J. R.

Dinah Johnson

Quinnie
Blue

paintings by James Ransome

Henry Holt and Company

NEW YORK

Hattie Lottie Annie Quinnie Blue—
that's the rhythm that the rain made
dancing on top of your tin roof
during Carolina summer showers.
Did you learn your long, happy name
listening, singing, dancing with the rain?

Grandma, I hope that it's okay with you
if I just call you Quinnie Blue. . . .

Quinnie Blue, did you like to go
to the crab crack?
People standing round the table
with a big pot in the middle.
Crabs climbing the air.
People eating all day long.

Quinnie Blue, I bet you walked barefoot outdoors.
Did you hear your mama say, "Girl, put some shoes on your feet
or you might get worms"?
Or did she say, "Doesn't the green grass feel good tickling your toes"?

Quinnie Blue, were you brave enough
to walk right up the church aisle
with everyone staring at you,
saying "Tell it girl" and "Hallelujah"?

I can hear you reciting your poem for Easter Sunday. And you'd be proud of me, reciting Mr. Dunbar's "Christmas is a-comin'."

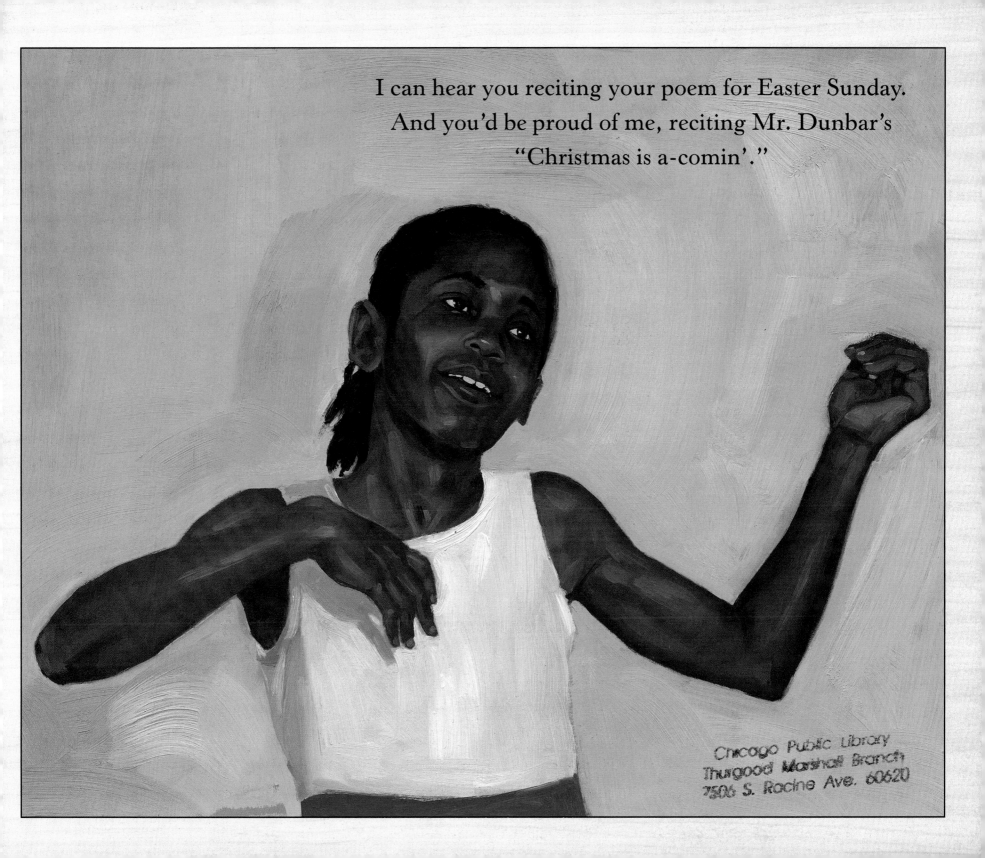

Mama says you were thankful for all the little somethings
that you found in your stocking—
a rag doll, a juicy orange,
the red gloves that Miss Beatrice crocheted just for you.
Mama says I should be thankful too.

Quinnie Blue,
did your mama teach you about the family tree?
You must have had plenty of company,
with Aunt Lee over yonder,
Cousin Niani on the same road,
Uncle Douglas round the corner.
And who did you look like on that family tree?
Did you have a smile like your brother Richie?
Did you have ears like your sister Sonia?

Quinnie Blue, did you wear your hair in braids like mine?
Wasn't it hard to sit for such a long time
while your mama made you look like a princess?
Did you learn to plait by braiding the pine needles
that made a blanket on the ground?

Skipping down the sweet-grass path,
I bet you sang out for your pony, Sassafras.
You'd kiss her nose and on you'd go—

because your afternoons wouldn't be the same
without playing your favorite hand-clap game
with Marie and Dianne.

Then you were off again,
running down the path to the tree with the swing,
where your daddy pulled you way, way back
and sent you soaring up into the air . . .

. . . up where the wind sang
Hattie Lottie Annie Quinnie Blue.
Your very own sassy womanchild song.

Grandma, I'm glad that I'm named after you—

Hattie Lottie Annie Quinnie Blue.

Author's Note

My great-grandmothers—Hattie, Lottie, Annie, and Quinnie—lived in Holly Hill, South Carolina, the place with tall pines and pecan trees, where it's warm almost all year long. I knew all four of my great-grandmothers, but I knew Quinnie the best. I spent many hours on her front porch. Sometimes I saw her fishing pole leaning up against one end of the porch, waiting for her to go down to Four Holes Swamp. On the other end of the porch, always, was her rocking chair. There she would sit smoking her pipe. While she sat, her great-grandchildren stood behind her and braided her long yellow-gray hair. And we listened to her stories about girlhood escapades, about her God, about the people who were in her heart, about the babies she delivered all over the county. Sometimes when we, her family, are feeling as helpless as babies, or even strong and new, we listen for the laughter and wisdom of Quinnie Wright Blue.

Henry Holt and Company, LLC, Publishers since 1866

115 West 18th Street, New York, New York 10011

Henry Holt is a registered trademark of Henry Holt and Company, LLC

Published in Canada by Fitzhenry & Whiteside Ltd., 195 Allstate Parkway, Markham, Ontario L3R 4T8.

Library of Congress Cataloging-in-Publication Data

Johnson, Dinah.

Quinnie Blue / Dinah Johnson; paintings by James Ransome.

Summary: A young girl wonders about the activities of her grandmother Quinnie Blue when she was little.

[1. Grandmothers—Fiction. 2. Afro-Americans—Fiction.] I. Ransome, James, ill. II. Title.

PZ7.J631634Qu 1999 [E]—dc21 98-47830

ISBN 0-8050-4378-0 /First Edition—2000 / Designed by Martha Rago

The artist used oil on canvas and acrylic on wood to create the illustrations for this book.

Printed in the United States of America on acid-free paper. ∞

1 3 5 7 9 10 8 6 4 2